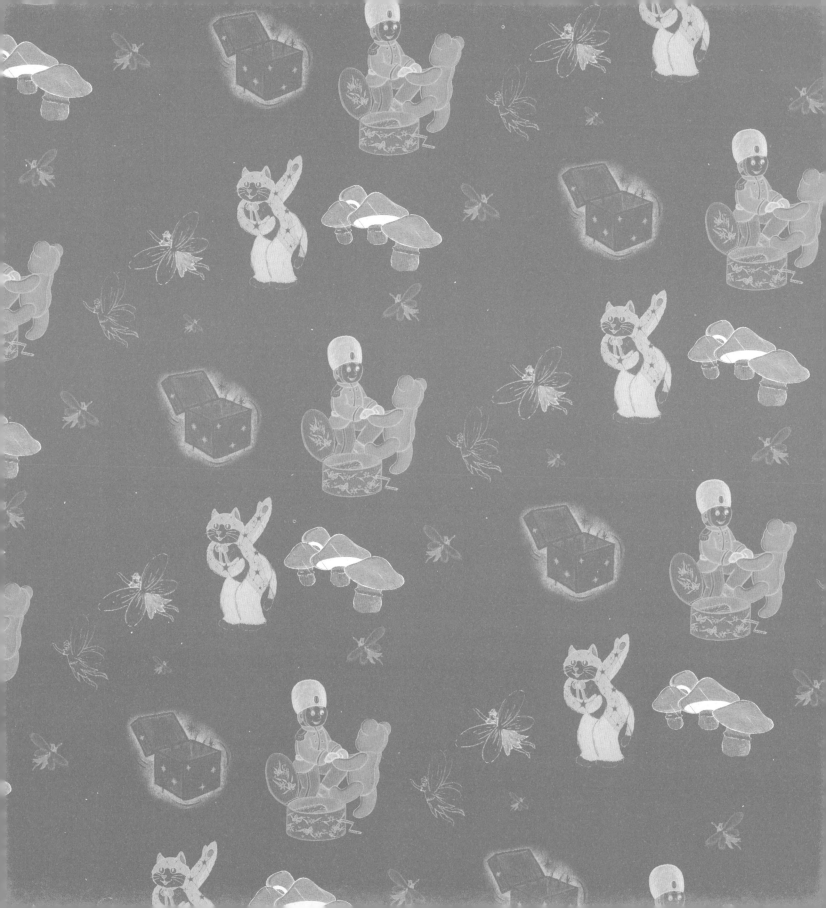

Jinky the Jumping Frog

~ & ~

Thirteen O'clock

Published in 2004 by Mercury Books London
20 Bloomsbury Street, London WC1B 3JH

© text copyright Enid Blyton Limited
© copyright original illustrations, Hodder and Stoughton Limited
© new illustrations 2004 Mercury Books London

Designed and produced for Mercury Books
by Open Door Limited, Langham, Rutland

Title: Jinky the Jumping Frog & Thirteen O'clock
ISBN: 1 904668 35 6

Jinky the Jumping Frog
~ & ~
Thirteen O'clock

MERCURY BOOKS
LONDON

Jinky the Jumping Frog

J inky was a little green jumping frog who lived in the toy cupboard with all the other toys. He had a spring inside him that made him able to jump high up in the air, and he often frightened the toys with his enormous jumps. He didn't mean to frighten them, but, you see, he couldn't walk or run, so his only way of getting about was to jump.

"I'm sorry if I startle you," he said to the angry toys. "Please try and get used to my big hops. I can't do anything else, you see."

The toys thought he was silly. He was a shy little frog, and he didn't say much, so the toys thought him stupid. They left him out of all their games at night, and he was often very lonely when he sat in a corner of the toy cupboard and watched the toys playing with one of the nursery balls.

Now the prettiest and daintiest of all the toys was Silvertoes, the fairy doll. She was perfectly lovely, and she had a silver crown on her head, a frock of finest gauze that stood out all round her, a pair of shining silver wings, and a little silver wand, which she always carried in her right hand. Everyone loved her, and the green frog loved her most of all.

But she wouldn't even look at him! He had once made her jump by hopping suddenly down by her, and she had never forgiven him. So Jinky watched her from a distance and wished and wished she would smile at him just once. But she never did.

One night there was a bright moon outside, and the brownie who lived inside the apple tree just by the nursery window came and called the toys.

"Let's all go out into the garden and dance in the moonlight," he said. "It's lovely and warm, and we could have a fine time together."

Out went all the toys through the window! They climbed down the apple tree, and slid to the grass below. Then they began to dance in the moonlight. They all took partners except the green frog, who was left out. He sat patiently on the grass, watching the other toys, and wishing that he could dance too.

There was such a noise of talking and laughing that no-one noticed a strange throbbing sound up in the sky. No-one, that is, except the green frog. He heard it and he looked up. He saw a bright silver aeroplane, about as big as a rook, circling round and round above the lawn.

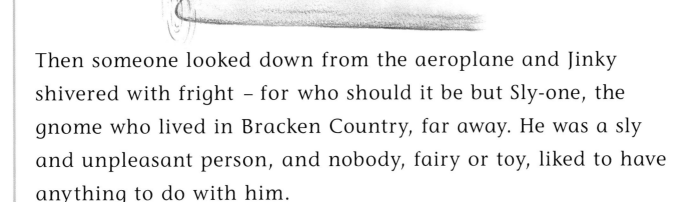

Then someone looked down from the aeroplane and Jinky shivered with fright – for who should it be but Sly-one, the gnome who lived in Bracken Country, far away. He was a sly and unpleasant person, and nobody, fairy or toy, liked to have anything to do with him.

"I wonder what he wants to come here for to-night!" said Jinky to himself. "He's up to some mischief, I'm sure!"

He was! He suddenly swooped down in his aeroplane, landed near the toys, ran up to the fairy doll, snatched her away from the teddy bear who was dancing with her, and ran off with her to his aeroplane!

How she screamed! "Help! Help! Oh, please save me, toys!"

The toys were so astonished that they stood and gaped at the bold gnome. He threw the fairy doll into his aeroplane, jumped in himself, and away he went into the air! Then the toys suddenly saw what was happening, and began to shout.

"You wicked gnome! Bring her back at once! We'll put you in prison if you don't!"

The gnome felt quite safe in the air. He circled round and round the toys and bent over the side of his aeroplane to laugh at them.

"Ha, ha!" he said. "Put me in prison, did you say? Well, come and catch me!"

To the great anger of the toys he flew very low indeed, just above their heads. The teddy bear, who was tall, tried to jump up and hang on to the aeroplane, but he couldn't quite reach it. He was in despair.

"Whatever shall we do?" he cried to the toys. "We can't possibly rescue the fairy doll in that horrid aeroplane."

"Ha, ha!" laughed the gnome again, swooping down to the toys – and just at that moment the green frog saw his chance! He would do a most ENORMOUS jump and see if he could leap right on to the aeroplane.

He jumped. My goodness me, what a leap that was! You should have seen him! He jumped right up into the air,  and reached out his front feet for the aeroplane. And he just managed it! He hung on the tail of the plane, and then managed to scramble up. The gnome had not seen him.

The toys were too astonished to say a word. They stood with open mouths looking up at the brave green frog, and he signed to them to say nothing about him. He thought that if the gnome did not know he was there he might be able to rescue the fairy doll without much difficulty.

The gnome flew off in his aeroplane. He wanted to reach Bracken Cottage that night, and he meant to marry the fairy doll in the morning. He thought it would be lovely to have such a pretty creature cooking his dinner and mending his clothes.

The frog crouched down on the tail of the aeroplane. It was very cold there, but he didn't mind. He was simply delighted to think that he would have a chance to do something for the pretty fairy doll.

At last Sly-One arrived at Bracken Cottage. He glided down and landed in the big field at the back of his house. Out he jumped, and turned to the fairy doll, who was cold, frightened and miserable.

"Wait here a minute and I'll just go and unlock the door," he said. "Then I'll come back and fetch you." He ran off – and as soon as he had gone the green frog hopped down into the seat beside the fairy doll.

She nearly screamed with fright, but he stopped her. "Sh!" he said. "It's only me, Jinky the jumping frog. I've come to save you. Do you think we can fly back in this aeroplane?"

"Oh, Jinky, I'm so glad to see you," sobbed the poor doll. "Look, you jerk that handle up, and the aeroplane should fly up into the air."

Jinky jerked the handle in front of him, but nothing happened. The gnome had stopped the engine and, of course, it wouldn't move. Jinky was in despair. He didn't in the least know how to fly the plane, and he was terribly afraid that if it did begin to fly there would be an accident.

"It's no good," he said, hopping out of the seat. "I can't make it go. Come on, fairy doll, get out, and jump on my back. I'll leap off with you, and perhaps we can escape that way."

"Take the handle out of the aeroplane," said the doll. "Then the nasty gnome can't fly after us in it. He won't be able to make it go up!"

"Good idea!" said the frog, and he tore off the handle. He put it into his mouth, for he was afraid to throw it anywhere in case the gnome found it again. He thought he would carry it a little way and then throw it into a bush. The fairy doll climbed on to his back, and held tight.

"Now please, don't be frightened," said the jumping frog. "I shall jump high, but you will be quite safe. I can't walk or run, you know."

"I shan't be frightened," said the fairy doll, clinging to his back. "I think you are the dearest, bravest, handsomest, strongest frog that I ever saw!"

"Well! How Jinky swelled with pride when he heard that! He looked behind him to see that the gnome was still far away – but, oh my goodness, he was running back from his cottage at top speed, for he had seen the doll get out of the aeroplane!

Jinky wasted no time but leapt high into the air and down again. Again and again he jumped, and each jump took him further away from the gnome, who had gone to his aeroplane to fly after them.

When he found that the starting handle had gone, he was very angry. He jumped out of the plane and ran to his garage. He opened the doors, and in a few moments Jinky heard the sound of a car engine roaring.

"Oh, my!" he thought in dismay. "If he comes after me in the car I shan't have any chance at all!"

On he went, leaping as far as he could each time. The fairy doll clung to him, and called to him to go faster still. Behind them came the gnome's car, driven at a fearful speed.

Then, crash! There came a tremendous noise, and Jinky turned round to see what had happened. The gnome had driven so fast round a corner that he had gone smash into a tree, and his car was broken to pieces. Sly-One jumped out unhurt, very angry indeed. He shook his fist at the jumping frog, and looked at his broken car.
Then he ran to a cottage nearby and thumped at the door.

The sleepy gnome came, and asked him what he wanted. "Lend me your bicycle," demanded the gnome. "I want to chase a wicked frog."

The goblin brought it out and the gnome jumped into the saddle. Off he pedalled at a furious rate after the frog and the doll.

"He's got a bicycle now!" shouted the fairy doll to Jinky. "Oh, hurry up, hurry up!" Jinky jumped as fast as he could, but the doll was heavy and he began to be afraid that he would never escape. Behind him came the gnome on the bicycle, ringing his bell loudly all the time.

Suddenly the frog came to a village, and in the middle of the street stood a policeman with red wings. He held out his hand to stop Jinky and the doll, but with a tremendous jump the frog leapt right over him and was at the other end of the village before the angry policeman knew what had happened. Then he heard the loud ringing of Sly-One's bicycle bell, and turned to stop the gnome. He held out his hand sternly.

But the gnome couldn't and wouldn't stop! He ran right into the astonished policeman, and knocked him flat on his face. Bump! The gnome flew off his bicycle and landed right in the middle of the duck pond nearby. The bicycle ran off by itself and smashed against a wall.

How angry that policeman was! He jumped to his feet and marched over to the gnome. "I arrest you for not stopping when I told you to, and for knocking me down," he said.

But the gnome slipped away from him, and ran down the street after the doll and the frog. The policeman ran after him, and off went the two, helter-skelter down the road.

The frog had quite a good start by now, and he was leaping for all he was worth. The doll was telling him all that had happened, and when he heard how the gnome had run into the policeman, he laughed so much that he got a stitch in his side and had to stop to rest.

"Oh, don't laugh!" begged the doll. "It really isn't funny. Do get on Jinky."

His stitch was soon better, and on he went again, while some way behind him panted the gnome and the policeman.

The frog felt sure he could jump faster than the gnome could run, so he wasn't so worried as he had been. For two more hours he jumped and jumped, and at last he came to the place where the toys had been dancing last night. They had all gone back to the nursery, very sad because they felt sure that the fairy doll and the frog were lost forever.

The frog jumped in at the window, and the fairy doll slid off his back. How the toys shouted with glee! How they praised the brave frog, and begged his pardon for the unkind things they had said and done to him. And you should have seen his face when the fairy doll suddenly threw her arms round his neck and kissed him! He was so pleased that he jumped all round the room for joy.

Suddenly there was a shout outside. It was the gnome still running, and the policeman after him! The gnome was so angry that he meant to run into the nursery and fight the jumping frog!

Then teddy bear did a clever thing. He put an empty box just underneath the window, and waited by it with the lid in his hands. The gnome jumped through the window straight into the box, and the bear clapped the lid down on him!

When the policeman came into the room too,

21

the bear bowed gravely to him and handed him the box neatly tied round with string.

"Here is your prisoner," he said. "Please take him away, he is making such a noise."

The surprised policeman thanked the bear, bowed to the toys, and went out of the window again. Then the toys sat down and had a good laugh, but the one who laughed the loudest of all was Jinky, the little green frog!

Thirteen O'clock

Once upon a time Sandy was walking home from school when he saw an extra fine dandelion clock. "What a beauty!" he said, picking it with its stalk. "I wonder if it will tell me the right time."

He blew it – puff! A cloud of white fluffy seeds flew away. There were plenty left on the clock. He blew again– puff! More fluff flew away on the breeze. Puff! Puff! Puff! He counted as he blew.

"One o'clock! Two o'clock! Three! Four! Five! Six o'clock! Seven! Eight! Nine! Ten! Eleven o'clock! Twelve o'clock! Thirteen o'clock!"

At the thirteenth puff there was no fluff left on the dandelion clock at all. It was just an empty stalk.

And then things began to happen. A noise of little voices was heard, and Sandy looked down at his feet. Round him was a crowd of pixies, shouting loudly.

"Did you say thirteen o'clock? Hi, did you say thirteen o'clock?"

"Yes" said Sandy, in astonishment. "The dandelion clock said thirteen o'clock."

"Oh my goodness me, thirteen o'clock only happens once in a blue moon!" cried the biggest pixie. "Whatever shall we do?"

"Why, what's the matter?" asked Sandy. "What are you so upset about?"

"Don't you know?" shouted all the pixies together. "Why, at thirteen o'clock all the witches from Witchland fly on broomsticks, and if they see any elf, pixie, brownie or gnome out of Fairyland they catch them and take them away. Oh dear, goodness gracious, whatever shall we do?"

Sandy felt quite alarmed. "Do they take little boys, too?" he asked.

"We don't know, but they might," answered the biggest pixie. "Hark! Can you hear the Witches' Wind blowing?"

Sandy listened. Yes, a wind was blowing up, and it sounded a funny sort of wind, all whispery and strange.

"That's the wind the witches use to blow their broomsticks along," said the pixies. "Little boy, you'd better run home quickly."

But Sandy wasn't going to leave the little pixies alone. They were frightened, so he felt he must stay and look after them. "I'll stay with you," he said. "But do you think you could make me as small as you, because if I'm as big as this the witches will see me easily and catch me."

"That's easy to do," said the biggest pixie. "Shut your eyes, put your hands over your ears and whisper 'Hoona-looki-allo-pie' three times to yourself. Then you'll be as small as we are.

When you want to get big again do exactly the same, but say the magic words backwards."

Sandy felt excited. He shut his eyes and covered his ears with his hands. Then he whispered the magic words three times – and lo and behold, when he opened his eyes again he was as small as the pixies! They crowded round him, laughing and talking.

"I am Gobbo," said the biggest one, "and this is my friend, Twinkle."

Sandy solemnly shook hands with Gobbo and Twinkle. Then, as the wind grew louder, the pixies crowded together in alarm, and looked up at the sky.

"Where shall we go to hide?" said Twinkle. "Oh, quick, think of somewhere, somebody, or the witches will be along and will take us prisoners!"

Everybody thought hard, and then Sandy had a good idea.

"As I came along I noticed an old saucepan thrown away in the hedge," he said. "Let's go and find it and get under it. It will hide us all beautifully."

Off went all the pixies, following Sandy. He soon found the saucepan, and by pushing hard they managed to turn it upside-down over them, so that it quite hid them. There was a hole in the side out of which they could peep. "I've dropped my handkerchief," suddenly cried Twinkle, pointing to where a little red hanky lay on the ground some way off. "I must go and get it."

"No, don't," said Gobbo. "You'll be caught. The witches will be along any minute now. Hark how the wind is blowing!"

"But I must get it!" cried Twinkle. "If I don't the witches will catch sight of it out there, and down they'll all come to see what it is. Then they'll sniff pixies nearby and come hunting under this saucepan for us."

"Ooooooooh!" groaned all the pixies, in fright. "Well, go and get it quickly!" said Gobbo to Twinkle. "Hurry up!"

Twinkle crept out from under the saucepan and everybody watched him anxiously. The wind grew louder and louder and all the tall grasses swayed like trees in the wind. Then there came a sort of voice in the wind and Sandy listened to hear what it said.

"The witches are coming, the witches are coming!" it said, in a deep-down, grumbling sort of voice, rushing into every hole and corner. Sandy peeped through the hole in the saucepan to see what Twinkle was doing. He was dodging here and there between the grasses. At last he reached the place where his red handkerchief lay, and he picked it up and put it into his pocket.

And then, oh my goodness, the pixies in the saucepan saw the first witches coming! They shouted to Twinkle, and he looked up in the sky. There they were, three witches in pointed hats and long cloaks, sitting on long broomsticks, flying through the cloudy sky.

"Quick, Twinkle, quick!" yelled Sandy and the pixies. How they hoped the witches wouldn't see him! He crouched down under a yellow buttercup till they were past, and then began to run to the saucepan.

"There are two more witches coming!" shouted the pixies, pointing. Sure enough, two more could be seen in the windy sky, much lower down than the others. Twinkle crept under a green stinging-nettle and stayed there without movement till the witches had gone safely by.

"Poor Twinkle! He will be stung!" said Gobbo, sadly. When the two witches were past Twinkle ran from beneath the nettle straight to the saucepan and crept underneath in safety. How glad all the pixies were! They crowded round him and stroked his nettle-stung hands and face.

"Never mind, Twinkle, you're safe here," they said.

"Look at all the witches now!" cried Sandy peeping through the hole. "Oh my! What a wonderful sight! I'm glad I'm seeing this."

It certainly was a marvellous sight! The sky was simply full of flying witches, and some of them had black cats sitting in front of them on the broomsticks. The cats coiled their tails round the sticks and held on like monkeys. It was funny to see them.

"Does this always happen at thirteen o'clock?" asked Sandy.

"Always," said Twinkle, solemnly. "But thirteen o'clock only happens once in a blue moon, as I told you before. The moon must have been blue this month. Did you notice it?"

"Well, no, I didn't," said Sandy.
"I'm nearly always in bed when it's
moonlight. Oh I say! Look! One of the
witches has lost her black cat!"

The pixies peeped out of the hole in the
saucepan. Sure enough, one of the black
cats had tumbled off its broomstick.
It had tried to be clever and wash
itself on the broomstick, and had
lost its hold and tumbled off. It
was falling through the air, and
the witch was darting down with
her broomstick, trying her best
to catch it.

She just managed to grab hold of
the cat before it fell on the ground –
but her broomstick was smashed

to pieces, and the witch rolled over and over on the grass, holding the cat safely in her arms. She sat up and looked round. When she saw her broken broomstick she began to howl.

"It's broken. It's broken! I'll never be able to fly back home! Boo hoo hoo!"

Sandy was frightened to see the witch rolling over and over. He thought she would be sure to hurt herself. He was a very kind-hearted boy, and he longed to go and ask her if she was all right. He began to squeeze himself under the saucepan, meaning to go and see if the witch was hurt. But the pixies tried to pull him back.

"Don't go, don't go," they whispered, for the witch was quite near. "She'll change you into a black-beetle."

"Why should she?" asked Sandy. "I'm going to be kind to her. Besides, she's got a nice face, rather like my granny's – I'm sure she isn't a bad witch."

He wriggled himself away from the hands of the pixies and ran over to the witch. She was sitting down on the grass crying big tears all down her cheeks. The cat was on her lap, still looking frightened.

The witch was most surprised to see him. Sandy stopped just by her. She had a very tall pointed hat, a long cloak round her shoulders, with silver suns, moons and stars all over it. The cat arched its back and spat angrily at the little boy.

"Excuse me," said Sandy, politely. "I saw you roll over on the ground when your broomstick broke, and I came to see if you were hurt."

"Well," said the witch, holding out her left hand, "I'm not much hurt – but my hand is a bit cut. I must have hit it against a stone when I rolled over."

"I'll tie it up for you with my handkerchief."
Said Sandy. "It's quite clean."

The witch looked more astonished than ever. She held out her hand and Sandy tied it up very neatly.

"Thank you," said the witch. "That's most kind of you. Oh dear – just look at my poor broomstick – it's broken in half! I shall never get back to Witchland again!"

Sandy looked at the broomstick. The broom part was all right, but the stick was broken. Sandy felt in his pocket to see if he had brought his knife with him. Yes, he had!

"I'll cut you another stick from the hedge," he said. "Then you can fit it into the broomhead and use it to fly away with!"

"You're the cleverest, kindest boy I ever met!" said the witch. "Thank you so much! Most people are afraid of witches, you know, because they think we will change them into black-beetles, or something – but that's an old-fashioned idea. The old witches were like that but nowadays we witches are decent folk, making magic spells that will do no-one any harm at all."

"Well, I'm glad to hear that!" said Sandy, hoping that the pixies under the saucepan were hearing it, too. He went to the hedge and cut another stick for the witch. He fitted it neatly into the broomhead and threw away the broken stick. The witch was very pleased.

She said a magic spell over it to make it able to fly. Then she turned to Sandy.

"Won't you have a ride with me?" she asked. "It is great fun. I will see that you are safe."

"Ooh, I'd love a ride!" cried Sandy, in delight. "But you are sure you won't take me away to Witchland?"

"I told you that witches don't do horrid things now," said the witch. "Do I look like a nasty witch?"

"No, you don't," said Sandy. "Well, I'll come for a ride – I'd love to! I'll be awfully late for my dinner but an adventure like this doesn't come often!"

He perched himself on the broomstick, behind the witch, who took her black cat on her knee. Just as they were about to set off, there came a great clatter, and the saucepan nearby was overturned by the pixies. They streamed out, shouting and calling.

"Take us for a ride, too! Take us for a ride, too!"

The witch looked at them in amazement. She had no idea that any pixies were near. She laughed when she saw where they had been hiding.

"Climb up on the stick," she said. "I'll give you a ride, too!"

Goodness, there wasn't room to put a blade of grass on that broomstick after all the pixies had climbed up on it! What a squash there was, to be sure!

The witch called out a string of magic words and the broomstick suddenly flew up into the air with a jerk. Sandy held on tightly. The pixies yelled in delight and began to sing joyfully. All the other witches flying high in the sky laughed to see such a crowded broomstick. Sandy did enjoy himself. He was very high up, and the wind whistled in his ears and blew his hair straight back from his head.

"Now we're going down again!" said the witch, and the broomstick swooped downwards. It landed gently and all the pixies tumbled off in a heap. Sandy jumped off and thanked the witch very much for such a lovely ride.

"I must go now," she said. "The hour of thirteen o'clock is nearly over and I must return to Witchland. Good-bye, kind little boy, and I'll give you another ride next time it's thirteen o'clock. If you wait for me here, I'll take you all the way to Witchland and back!"

Off she went, she and her black cat, and left Sandy standing on the grass, watching her fly away. The pixies waved to the witch and she waved back. "Well, that was an adventure!" cried the pixies. "We'll never be afraid of witches again, that's certain! Hooray!"

"I wonder what the time is," said Sandy. "What comes after thirteen o'clock? Is it fourteen o'clock?"

"Oh no!" said Twinkle. "Thirteen o'clock just comes and goes. It isn't any time really. It always comes after twelve o'clock, but it's followed by one o'clock as if nothing had happened in between!"

Somewhere a church clock chimed the hour. Sandy listened. Then the clock struck one, and no more.

"One o'clock, one o'clock!" cried the pixies their voices growing very small and faint. "Thirteen o'clock is over! Good-bye, good-bye!"

Sandy looked at them – they were vanishing like the mist, and in a moment or two he could see nothing of them. They just weren't there.

"I must make myself big again," he thought. He remembered the words quite well. He shut his eyes and covered up his ears. He had to say the magic words backwards, so he thought hard before he spoke.

"Pie-allo-looki-hoona!" he said. When he opened his eyes he was his own size again! He set off home, running as fast as he could, for he was afraid that his mother would be wondering where he was. He ran into the house and found his mother just putting out his dinner. She didn't seem to think he was late at all!

"You're just in nice time," she said to Sandy. "Good boy! You must have come straight from school without stopping!" "But mother – ever such a lot has

happened since I left school," said Sandy in surprise. "I'm dreadfully late!"

"No, darling, it's only just gone one o'clock," said his mother, looking at the clock.

"Didn't you have thirteen o'clock, too, this morning?" asked Sandy, sitting down to his dinner.

"What are you talking about?" said his mother with a laugh. "Thirteen o'clock! Whoever heard of that? That only happens in Fairyland, once in a blue moon, I should think!"

Sandy thought about it. Perhaps it was true – perhaps thirteen o'clock belonged to the fairies, and not to the world of boys and girls. How lucky he had been to have that one magic hour of thirteen o'clock with the pixies and the witch. And next time it was thirteen o'clock he was going to ride on a broomstick again. Oh, what fun!

"I do hope it will be thirteen o'clock again soon," he said.

"Eat up your dinner and don't talk nonsense!" said his mother, laughing.

But it wasn't nonsense, was it? Sandy is going to blow all the dandelion clocks he sees so that he will know when it is thirteen o'clock again. If you blow them too, you may find that magic hour as well!

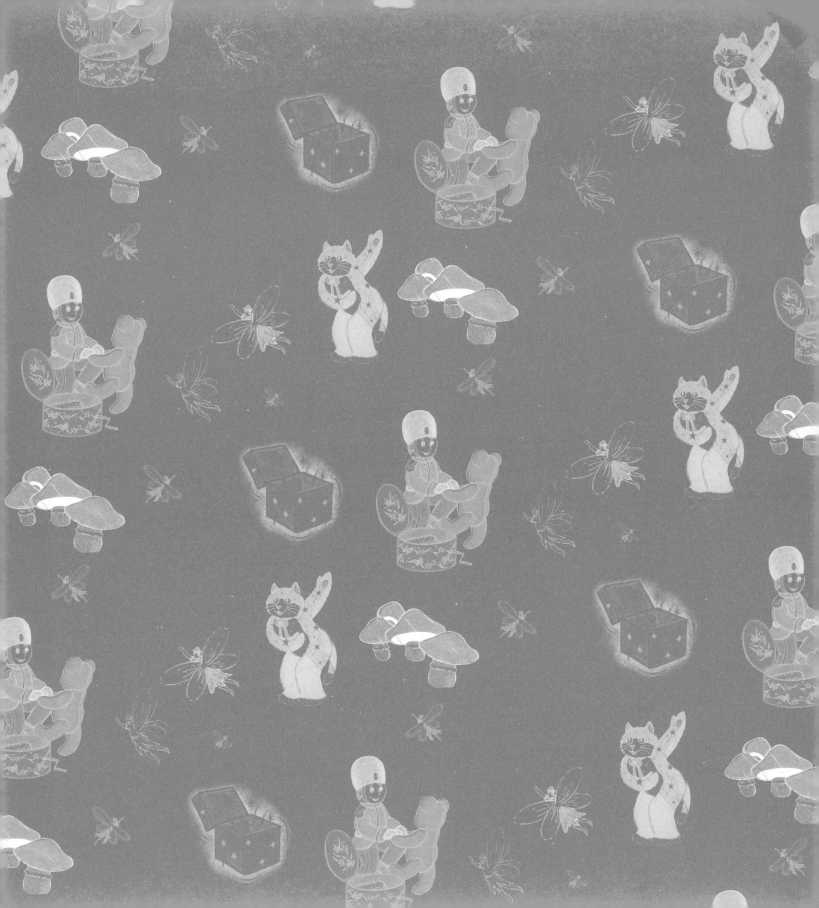

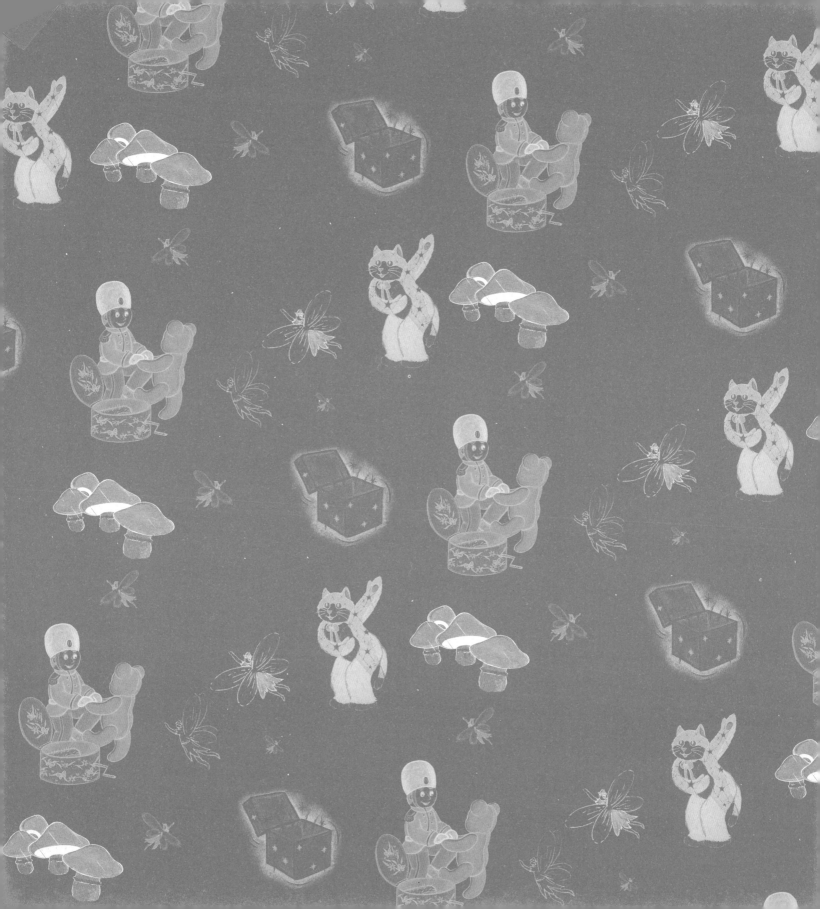